TIMBERWOLF
Chase

TIMBERWOLF
Chase

Sigmund Brouwer
illustrations by Dean Griffiths

ORCA BOOK PUBLISHERS

Library and Archives Canada Cataloguing in Publication

Brouwer, Sigmund, 1959-
Timberwolf chase / Sigmund Brouwer; illustrations by Dean Griffiths.
(Orca echoes)
(Howling Timberwolves series)

ISBN 10: 1-55143-548-9 / ISBN 13: 978-1-55143-548-0

I. Title. II. Series. III. Series: Brouwer, Sigmund, 1959- .
Howling Timberwolves series.
PS8553.R68467T543 2006   jC813'.54   C2006-903012-X

First published in the United States, 2006
Library of Congress Control Number: 2006927087

Summary: In this first book in the Timberwolves series, a new player moves to the small town
of Howling, and Johnny Maverick must find a way to make him part of the team.

Orca Book Publishers gratefully acknowledges the support for its publishing programs provided
by the following agencies: the Government of Canada through the Book Publishing Industry
Development Program and the Canada Council for the Arts, and the Province of British
Columbia through the BC Arts Council and the Book Publishing Tax Credit.

*Orca Book Publishers is dedicated to preserving the environment and has
printed this book on Forest Stewardship Council® certified paper.*

Design and typesetting by Doug McCaffry
Cover and interior illustrations by Dean Griffiths
Author photo by Reba Baskett

ORCA BOOK PUBLISHERS
PO BOX 5626, Stn. B
Victoria, BC Canada
V8R 6S4

ORCA BOOK PUBLISHERS
PO BOX 468
Custer, WA USA
98240-0468

www.orcabook.com
Printed and bound in Canada.
15 14 13 12 • 6 5 4 3

*To Sylvie Tarnowsky and her
beloved Jerry—D.G.*

CHAPTER ONE

Johnny Maverick thought he saw something move inside his hockey bag. Things in hockey bags should not move, he told himself.

Johnny was in the dressing room with the rest of the players on the Howling Timberwolves hockey team. It was the first practice of the year. His hockey bag was open on the floor in front of him. He was ready to put on his equipment for the practice.

But something in the bag had moved.

He leaned forward to look inside the bag. He pulled out a hockey glove. Something fell from the inside of the glove. It landed in the bag and disappeared.

"I hope I'm wrong," he said to himself. "I hope I didn't just see a—"

"Johnny!" Coach Smith said to him. "Are you listening?"

"Um, no," Johnny said. He was worried about his hockey bag. He looked in it again.

"Please," Coach Smith said, "look at me when I talk."

Johnny looked up. Everyone on the team was staring at him. Twelve players. All of them lived in or near a town called Howling. It was a small town. There were not a lot of hockey players for this team. They needed everybody they could get.

"Coach," Johnny said. "My mom made me keep my hockey equipment in the storage shed all summer. She thinks hockey equipment smells bad."

"She's right," Coach Smith said.

"That means I might have a problem," Johnny said. He looked back into the bag. He hoped the thing in the bag wasn't what he thought it was.

3

"The problem is you weren't listening," Coach Smith told Johnny. "Look at me when I'm talking. Please. I don't want to say it again."

"But—"

"No buts," Coach Smith said. "I'm the coach and I need to talk to the whole team."

"But—"

"Not another word, Johnny. Please. You know I like you very much. But I would like to go just one hockey season without any trouble from you."

Johnny didn't say anything else. Even when he thought he heard something move in his hockey bag. But he was afraid to look down. Coach Smith didn't like it if he thought a player wasn't listening.

Coach Smith spoke to everybody. "We have a new player this year. His name is Tom Morgan."

Coach Smith pointed at a boy in the corner. The boy had brown hair and brown eyes. He wasn't smiling.

"Tom and his parents have just moved here from Toronto," Coach Smith said. "I hope you make him feel welcome."

Johnny felt something on the top of his foot. That made him look down.

He saw a mouse.

CHAPTER TWO

Yes, it was a mouse. A big fat mouse. From inside his hockey bag. The hockey bag that had been in the storage shed all summer.

The mouse stared at Johnny. Johnny stared back. Then the mouse tried to crawl up Johnny's pants.

Johnny yelled.

He kicked his foot straight up.

The mouse flew high into the air.

"Johnny!" Coach Smith said in an angry voice. "Pay attention."

Johnny was watching the mouse. He saw where it was going to land.

"Coach!" Johnny yelled.

But it was too late.

The mouse landed on Coach Smith's head.

Coach Smith frowned. He didn't know what had landed on his head.

But Johnny did.

Johnny wanted to help Coach Smith. He grabbed his hockey glove. Coach Smith was short, and Johnny knew he could reach the mouse on top of his head.

Johnny swung the glove at the mouse.

He missed the mouse.

But he didn't miss Coach Smith's head. He hit Coach Smith in the head with the hockey glove.

Something hairy landed on the floor.

Johnny yelled again. He wondered if he had knocked off Coach Smith's head. But right away Johnny saw that it wasn't Coach Smith's head. It was Coach Smith's hair.

Coach Smith wore a wig? Johnny never knew that.

He did now. So did the rest of the team.

Coach Smith's face turned red. It always did that when he was going to yell at Johnny.

"Are you crazy?" Coach Smith said. "Why did you hit me on the—"

Then Coach Smith noticed the wig on the floor. He reached up and touched his head. His fingers touched the skin of a bald head. His face began to turn purple. The coach's face only turned purple once or twice a season. It took something really, really bad to make Coach Smith's face turn purple.

Coach Smith opened his mouth to really, really yell at Johnny.

Then he shut his mouth. A funny look crossed on his face. He looked down at his shirt. Johnny looked too. He noticed something move inside Coach Smith's shirt. A little bump that was moving.

So that's where the mouse went, Johnny told himself. It was in Coach Smith's shirt.

"It's a mouse," he told Coach Smith.

"A mouse? In my shirt?"

The bump moved again.

"A mouse," Johnny repeated. "From my hockey bag. You see, my mom put my equipment in the shed for the summer because it smells bad."

"A mouse!" Coach Smith started to hit himself to try to get the mouse.

The bump moved farther down Coach Smith's shirt. Right down to his belt buckle.

Coach Smith hopped and hopped. He hit himself harder. But he kept missing the mouse.

Coach Smith finally screamed and ran out of the room. Everyone heard his screaming as he ran down the hallway.

It was very quiet in the dressing room after that. Too quiet.

Johnny picked up Coach Smith's wig and dusted the dirt off.

"Hi," Johnny said to the new player as he dusted the wig clean. "Welcome to the Howling Timberwolves. As you can see, this team is like a big happy family."

Chapter Three

"Run everyone!" Tom Morgan yelled. "Danger!"

It was the day after the practice. Johnny Maverick was on the playground during recess. He was talking to his friend Stu Duncan about the hockey practice and the mouse. And how Coach Smith didn't think any of it was funny.

"It's a whale!" Tom yelled again. Tom was near Johnny and Stu. Tom was pointing at Stu as he yelled. "Everyone! Run away!"

"What is the new kid yelling about?" Johnny asked.

"I think he's calling me a whale," Stu said. "In front of everyone in the school."

"No, everyone, wait!" Tom yelled. "Whale season just opened. Get me a harpoon. I'll save us."

"Hey," Johnny said to Tom, "do you think you're funny?"

"No," Tom said. "I think Stu is fat. And he looks like a whale."

"Fat?" Stu said. He turned to Johnny. "Do I look fat? Don't lie to me. We're friends. I can take the truth."

"No," Johnny told his friend. "You don't look fat. Chubby. But not fat."

"Do I have a blowhole on my back?" Stu asked. He took off his jacket and handed it to Johnny. "Give me a second to get my shirt off. You can have a good look at my back and tell me."

"Please stop," Johnny said. "If you have as much hair on your back as your dad, I will throw up. Besides I would have remembered a blowhole from all the times we went swimming in the summer. I do remember bubbles in the water, but I don't think they came from your back."

"See," Stu told the new kid. "I'm not fat. I'm chubby. And I don't have a blowhole, even though sometimes I can make bubbles in the water. So I can't be a whale. Maybe you need glasses."

"Maybe I need a better left winger than you," Tom said. "Yesterday in practice you should have scored five times with the great passes I gave you. But you missed all of them because you are too big and too slow."

"They were great passes," Stu said. "You are a very good hockey player, and we are happy to have you on the team. After only one practice, we all know you are the best player on the ice. Probably in the league. But you are still wrong about those passes."

"Wrong?" Tom asked.

"You said I missed five passes because I am too big and too slow," Stu said. "But I only missed *four* passes because I am big and slow. I missed the last pass because I was looking at the concession stand to see if they had any hotdogs left for after practice."

"You're not taking this seriously," Tom said. His face was tight with a frown.

"No," Stu said.

"My insults don't make you want to play better hockey? To try harder? To maybe start looking for passes instead of hotdogs?"

"Not really," Stu said. "I like hotdogs. Besides, your insults mean nothing to me. I've watched Oprah."

"Oprah?"

"Oprah," Stu said. "On TV. She had this episode about dealing with insults. I can't control what you say. Only how I react to it. Right, Johnny?"

"It was a good episode," Johnny said, "but not as good as the one about cute girls who think they are ugly. Remember that one blond girl who went to school with a paper bag over her head?"

"I do," Stu said. "She was really cute. I taped that episode."

"Listen to me!" Tom yelled. "This is not about Oprah!"

16

"Oh," Johnny said.

"Oh," Stu said.

"This is about winning hockey games. In Toronto, I was in the elite league. I am used to playing with great players. I'm not used to losing. And I don't play with wingers who check out the concession stand in the middle of practice."

"Welcome to the town of Howling," Johnny said. "Now you get to experience new things. Like how much fun it is to be part of a team. Even if we lose sometimes."

"Or worse, if the concession stand runs out of hotdogs," Stu said. "You have to take the good with the bad around here."

"You guys can't be serious for a second, can you?" Tom asked.

"One second at the most," Stu said very seriously.

Stu waited one second with that serious look on his face.

Then he smiled. "See, one second. Then all my seriousness is gone again. I also have a short attention span to go along with my chubbiness. It's part of my charm."

Tom didn't think that was funny. "Did your parents call you Stu because they knew you wouldn't be able to spell Stupid?"

"But I can spell idiot," Stu said. "Listen carefully. T — O — M."

"T — O — M?" Tom said. "That's how stupid you are. That doesn't spell idiot. That's how you spell Tom."

"Oh," Stu said. "Maybe I made a mistake because it is very hard to tell one from the other."

Some of the other kids who were listening began to laugh.

"That's it!" Tom said. "Nobody calls me an idiot. Let's fight. Right now."

CHAPTER FOUR

"I think he's serious," Stu said. "Look, he's making fists."

Tom, the new kid, had his fists up.

"This doesn't build teamwork," Johnny said to Tom. "I always want to hit him for all the bubbles in the water when we swim. But trust me, when you hit him, you just bounce off. I had to learn that the hard way."

"I don't care," Tom said. "He called me an idiot."

"Actually," Stu said, "it's more like you called yourself an idiot. Maybe you should punch yourself."

Tom glared at Stu. Tom kept his fists up and started circling Stu. "Come on. Fight. Or are you chicken?"

"Make up your mind," Stu said. "I can't be a whale *and* a chicken."

The kids around them laughed at this too. They all liked Stu.

"I don't know what school you came from," Johnny said to the new kid. "But here in Howling, it is not smart to fight. The teachers don't like it. You have to stay in after school. They call the parents. You have to apologize to each other, even though you don't mean it. Stuff like that."

"I don't care," Tom said. "He called me an idiot."

"And if you fight," Johnny said. "They might not let you play hockey in tomorrow's game. Grown-ups around here really don't like fights on the playground."

"Oh," Tom said.

Tom dropped his fists and stopped circling Stu.

Tom shook his head. "It's not worth missing a hockey game because of an ugly whale like you."

20

"Ugly hurts," Stu said. "I can't deny the chubby part, but ugly…"

Johnny finally got mad, even if Stu wasn't upset at the insults. It wasn't right for Tom to talk like this. Stu was Johnny's good friend. But when Johnny got mad, sometimes he said things that weren't smart.

"You just wait until tomorrow's game," Johnny said. "You'll see that Stu is a great hockey player. He might even score more goals than you."

"Sure," Tom said. "You bet. I'll wait. I'll even make sure to give him five more great passes. How about he promises to quit if he doesn't score a single goal?"

"How about just watch him score?" Johnny said.

Tom laughed a mean laugh and walked away.

"Why did you tell him I'm a great player?" Stu said to Johnny. "That's like telling people I'm skinny."

"You're my friend," Johnny said. "He made me mad."

"He made you lose half your brain," Stu said. "I hardly ever score goals, remember? What I do is squish people into the boards but only the ones who are too slow to move out of the way."

"Maybe tomorrow night you will get lucky and score some goals," Johnny said.

"Sure," Stu said, "and maybe the next time you drop a bowling ball on my foot, it won't hurt."

"That was two months ago and I already said sorry," Johnny said. "Some things you should just try to forget."

"And other things maybe I should just quit," Stu said. "Tom is right. I'm not good at hockey."

"You can't quit," Johnny Maverick said. "We have a small team in a small town. We need everybody."

"Then what should I do? You told him I was going to score more goals than him. It would be better if I pretended I was sick tomorrow night and didn't play."

"Don't worry," Johnny said. "We'll figure something out."

"You always say that," Stu said. "And you're always wrong."

"At least I never quit," Johnny said. "And neither should you."

Chapter Five

The Howling Timberwolves skated onto the ice to begin the third period. The score was four to three. Tom Morgan had scored all four of the Timberwolves' goals.

"Did you get lost?" Johnny said to Stu as they skated to the bench.

"Lost?"

"During the break you said you needed to ask your mom something and left the dressing room," Johnny said. "It sure took a long time for you to get back."

"I don't think you should worry about that," Stu said. "You better score a goal. Otherwise Tom will never let us forget about it."

"Me?" Johnny said. "How about you? Tom gave you five great passes. Your grandmother could have scored on those passes."

"I'll try my best," Stu said.

They got to the bench. Johnny sniffed the air.

"Hey," Johnny whispered. "I think I smell a hotdog."

"You do," Stu whispered back. "It's in my hockey glove."

"What!" Johnny whispered. "A hotdog!"

"After I talked to my mom, I went to the concession stand. The lineup was really long. I didn't have a chance to eat it. But I couldn't throw it away either."

"What are you going to do?" Johnny asked.

Stu didn't have a chance to answer. Coach Smith pointed at Stu and Tom. "On the ice, guys. Have a good shift."

Stu went on the ice with a hotdog in his hockey glove.

The referee dropped the puck to start the third period. Tom was a fast skater. He got the puck between the center line and the blue line.

"Go," Tom shouted at Stu.

The defenseman thought Tom was going to pass to Stu. Instead, Tom cut to the outside and skated around the defenseman. Now it was a two on one.

Tom waited until the last second. He pretended he was going to shoot. But he went around the net and came around the other side. By then Stu was in front of the net all alone.

Tom gave Stu a perfect pass.

Stu stopped the puck and tried to take a shot. As he swung his stick, the hotdog fell out of the bun. It fell out of his hockey glove and landed on the ice.

The goalie caught Stu's shot.

Tom was skating in for a rebound. He saw something on the ice. He fired it quickly into the back of the net. He raised his hands like he had scored a goal!

The referee blew his whistle.

The goalie looked in his glove. He saw a puck.

The goalie looked into the back of the net. He saw a hotdog.

Tom stopped beside Stu. Tom looked in the back of the net.

"Hey," Tom shouted at Stu. "Where did that come from?"

"Where did *what* come from?" Stu said. He was already trying to skate back to the bench.

Tom grabbed Stu's shoulders and spun him around and pointed him at the net.

"That," Tom said. "Look on the ice. In the net. It's a hotdog."

"Wow!" Stu said. "Someone must have thrown it on the ice."

Stu reached in behind the goalie with his hockey stick. He used his stick to pull the hotdog

toward him. He picked it up and bit into it.

"Not only that," Stu said, "but it's still hot. It could use some mustard, though."

"I can't believe this," Tom said.

"Really," Stu answered. He held out the hotdog. "Try it for yourself."

CHAPTER SIX

The next day, Johnny and Stu and the rest of the boys were running laps for gym class. Actually, for Johnny and Stu it was more like walking laps. Stu was not fast.

Tom came up alongside them.

"I thought I felt an earthquake," Tom said as he ran past them. "But then I saw that it was just Dumbo here."

"Hah, hah," Johnny said.

But Tom was already gone. Stu was not fast, and Johnny was staying with Stu.

"Remember, Oprah," Stu told Johnny.

"You mean my favorite episode?" Johnny asked. "The blond girl with the paper bag on her head?"

"No," Stu said. "The one where she said not to let another person's insults control you. Besides, it seems when you stick up for me, I'm the one who pays the price. Ignore Tom. Please."

It was hard for Johnny to do.

The next time Tom passed them, he said, "I could crawl faster than you, Stu. But then, so could a baby."

"Can I give him a wedgie?" Johnny asked Stu.

"You'd have to catch me," Tom said. "And I'm the fastest guy on the track."

To prove it, he sped up and was gone. But only for a few minutes. Soon he finished another lap and caught up to them again.

"Oink, oink," Tom said. "Oink, Oink."

"I thought I smelled a stinky pig," Johnny said to Stu. "I guess it's Tom."

"Ignore him," Stu said.

"Really," Tom said to Stu. "You should think about quitting hockey. For the good of the team. I've done three laps, and you're not even finished your first."

"We won last night," Johnny said to Tom.

"Yes, four to three," Tom said. "And I scored all four goals."

"Four great goals," Johnny said. "It really helped. That's why the team is just fine with Stu as part of it."

"Maybe as a water boy," Tom said. He ran fast again and left them behind.

A few minutes later, he caught up to them again.

"Four laps," Tom said. "Hurry up and finish one, whale boy. Outrunning you is as easy as beating a blind man."

"Johnny," Stu said as soon as Tom was gone again, "please help me remember my own advice."

"What's that?" Johnny said. "Never mix sardines with peanut butter?"

34

Stu had tried that once and didn't like it at all. He'd given it to his dog, and it made the dog throw up.

"No," Stu said, "my advice about ignoring insults. Tom is finally starting to bother me."

"I'm glad you said that," Johnny said. "I have an idea."

"What?"

"Remember he said outrunning you is as easy as beating a blind man?"

"You don't have to rub it in," Stu said.

"That gave me an idea."

"Your ideas always get me in trouble," Stu said.

But it was too late. Johnny yelled loud enough for everyone on the track to hear.

"Hey, Tom," Johnny yelled. "If Stu wanted, he could beat you in a race."

Stu elbowed Johnny. "Are you crazy?"

"Trust me," Johnny said. "Trust me and don't say a word."

Tom laughed and jogged back toward them. "Beat me in a race? Let's go. Right now."

"No," Johnny said. "He wants two weeks of special training. And I'll name the time and place."

"Whatever," Tom said. "He could have five years of training. He still wouldn't have a chance."

Other kids came closer to hear what the bet was. Johnny made sure to speak loud enough for everyone to hear.

"If Stu beats you in the race," Johnny said to Tom, "you have to wear a dress to the next hockey game."

"Sure," Tom said. "As long as he promises to quit hockey when I beat him."

"It's a deal," Johnny said.

Tom laughed and jogged away from them again.

"Like I told you," Stu said to Johnny, "your ideas always get me in trouble."

"Remember the two magic words," Johnny said.

"Johnny's crazy?"

"No," Johnny said. "Trust me."

CHAPTER SEVEN

Right after school that day, Johnny and Stu went straight to Veteran's Park in the middle of town.

A creek ran through the park. There was a narrow twisting path through the dense woods that grew alongside the creek.

Johnny took Stu to one end of the path.

"Remember I told Tom that I would name the time and place you would race him?" Johnny asked Stu.

"I'm trying to forget," Stu said.

Johnny pointed at the narrow twisting dirt path. Roots from trees stuck out of the ground in different places.

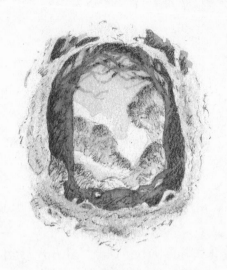

"This is the place," Johnny said. "What do you think?"

"Two things," Stu answered.

"Yes?"

"The first thing is that I think I will be lucky to make it to the other end without hurting myself," Stu said. "I'm chubby and wide. Tom is skinny and fast. I'll never beat Tom if we race on this path."

"We have two weeks to practice," Johnny said. "What is the second thing?"

"That I want to squeeze your throat until your eyeballs pop from your head," Stu said. "Everyone in the school knows about the bet you made. And now you want me to race that fast and skinny new kid on this path?"

"Trust me," Johnny said. "You might be chubby, but you are smart."

"Don't forget charming too."

"Yes. Smart and charming. But it's the smart part that will end up making Tom wear a dress to a hockey game."

"It would be nice if you started making sense," Stu said. "I may be smart, but my brain is stuck in a body that is big and slow."

"This afternoon we are going to run down the path slowly," Johnny said. "I want you to count how many steps it takes between each turn."

"Count."

"And memorize the count."

"Count and memorize? This is a race, remember, not a math class."

"Does anybody in the class get better grades than you in math?" Johnny asked.

"No." Stu said. "That's not bragging. It's just true."

"Then if we could turn the race into a math class," Tom said, "you would win, right?"

"Remember earlier I said my brain is stuck in a body that is big and slow?" Stu asked.

"Yes."

"And remember earlier I said it would be nice if you started making sense?" Stu asked.

"Yes."

"Now would be a good time to begin."

"Sure," Johnny told Stu. "I'll be happy to explain."

And he did.

CHAPTER EIGHT

Two weeks later, Johnny saw Tom in the hallway at school.

"Hey, new kid," Johnny said.

"Hey, loser," Tom answered. "When's that friend of yours going to lose his race so I can get him off our hockey team?"

"So you do remember the bet," Johnny said.

Kids in the hallway stopped to listen. Everybody knew about the bet.

"I'll race him any time, any place," Tom said. "That's the bet. When he loses, he promises to stop playing hockey for the Timberwolves. If you can call what he does on the ice playing hockey."

"Have you noticed he's a little faster on the ice these days?" Johnny asked.

Tom thought about it. "I hate to admit it, but yes, you're right."

"He's been working hard at his training," Johnny said. "It's not too late to call off the bet."

Tom shook his head. "He's still not fast enough to play the kind of hockey that I am used to. I don't want to be on the same team as a loser. Let's get the race over with so he'll quit."

"Hang on," Johnny said. "There is the other half of the bet."

"That if he wins the race, I have to wear a dress to the next hockey game."

"Yes," Johnny said. "That half."

"I'm not worried. What's the time and place?"

"The place," Johnny said, "is Veteran's Park. You know where that is, right?"

"In a town this small," Tom said, "it took only a day to know where everything is. I don't know how you can live here without going crazy."

"Easy. We find new kids from Toronto who promise to wear dresses to hockey games."

"Hah, hah," Tom said. "What time am I going to make your friend Stu look like a turtle?"

"Funny you should say that," Johnny said. "There is that story about the tortoise and the hare."

"It's a fairy tale," Tom said. "This is real life. What time?"

"Seven o'clock," Johnny answered. "Tonight."

Johnny knew the forecast was for a cloudy night. That would help Stu.

"Tonight?" Tom frowned.

Johnny shrugged. "Unless you're afraid of losing."

"Tonight," Tom said. "Seven o'clock. You better bring a big towel."

"Why?" Johnny said.

"For you and the whale boy to cry in," Tom said. "This is going to be like beating a blind man."

Johnny smiled. "I suppose you could say that."

43

CHAPTER NINE

Tom and Stu stood side by side where the path went into the woods. Johnny and the rest of the team were nearby to witness the race. But it was quite dark and they knew they would not actually be able to see what happened.

"Ready, set, go!" Johnny yelled.

"Out of my way, whale boy!" Tom said. He pushed Stu to the side and ran down the path.

Stu followed him into the trees.

Immediately, Johnny heard a loud *thunk*. Next came a loud *thump*.

"The first sound would be Tom hitting his head on a tree," Johnny said to the kids beside him in the park. "Then I think he fell."

"Maybe it was Stu hitting a tree," someone said. "Not Tom."

They heard a big "Oooooffff."

"Sorry, Tom!" they heard Stu say. "Didn't see you on the ground."

"Does that give you the answer?" Johnny said. "Stu stepped on Tom."

Next came a loud howling.

"That would be the thorn bushes," Johnny said to his friends. "The bushes are about ten more steps down the path. If Tom doesn't watch out, he's going to fall into the—"

A splash and more yelling reached them.

"Yup," Johnny said. "Right about there is where the path turns and if you miss the turn, you fall down the bank into the creek."

"How do you know this?" someone asked.

"Oh," Johnny said, "did Stu and I forget to mention that Stu has spent the last two weeks learning how to run down the path blindfolded?

Running here at night is easy for Stu."

They all heard more howling. Johnny had to wait until it was quieter to continue talking.

"That was probably the next set of thorn bushes," Johnny told them. "I hope Tom figures out that the faster he tries to go, the more trouble he will get into. There's another turn, and if you miss it you will—"

There was another big splash and yelling.

"Poor guy," Johnny said to the team. "Ahead of him is another big branch, four sets of thorn bushes and three more places to fall into the creek."

CHAPTER TEN

Johnny Maverick got to the dressing room early for the next hockey game. So did his friend Stu.

They were both wearing dresses. Johnny wore a blue dress. Stu wore a red dress. But they wore blue jeans underneath the dresses.

"Look," Stu said. He lifted his dress. He pulled out the front of his pants. "These are getting looser. I think I'm going to keep training every night after school. It seems to be helping."

"Good," Johnny said. He put his hockey bag on the floor. He sat on the bench. "I'll train with you. It really is making you a better player."

Stu put his hockey bag down and sat on the bench beside Johnny.

"Do you think Tom will wear a dress?" Stu asked Johnny.

"Yes," Johnny said. "I think he's the kind of guy who keeps his word. He's just a little too concerned about winning. And not concerned enough about being on a team."

"Thanks for helping me," Stu said.

"No problem," Johnny said. "I owe you one for dropping that bowling ball on your foot in the summer."

"I thought you said it was an accident."

"It could have been," Johnny answered. "But if you remember, you were winning before I dropped the ball on your foot. And after, you lost."

"Are you saying it wasn't an accident?"

Johnny grinned at his friend. "I'm saying that I like to win too. And I'm saying I'm glad I helped you with Tom to make up for hurting your toe."

Before Stu could answer, the door to the dressing room opened. It was Coach Smith.

Coach Smith stared at Johnny and Stu in their dresses.

"Is it Halloween and I forgot?" Coach Smith said.

"No," Johnny answered.

Coach Smith sighed. "Then whatever it is, I don't want to know."

Coach Smith pointed at Johnny's hockey bag on the floor. "Johnny, did you check your hockey bag for mice today?"

"Yes, I did," Johnny said. "How many more times are you going to ask me that?"

"Every practice and every game," Coach Smith said. "Who would think a mouse could poop so many times in a person's shirt?"

The door opened again.

"Hello, Coach," Tom said as he carried his hockey bag in to the dressing room.

Coach Smith stepped backward in surprise. "You're in a dress too?"

It was a dumb question, of course. Because the answer was yes. Tom was in a dress. This one was green. But he wasn't wearing blue jeans. It was quite a short dress with short sleeves. It showed the skin of his legs and arms. His legs were scratched. His arms were scratched. His face was scratched. And he had a big bump on his forehead.

"What happened to you?" Coach asked.

"The tortoise beat the hare," Tom said.

"Huh?" Coach said.

"You see, Johnny made a bet with me and—"

Tom stopped. He noticed that Stu and Johnny were wearing dresses too.

"Huh?" Tom said. "You guys didn't lose the bet. I did."

"Yes," Johnny said.

The door opened again before Johnny could finish answering. Two more guys on the hockey team entered. They were wearing dresses too.

"What is going on around here?" Coach Smith said. He looked at Johnny. "Whatever it is, it's your idea, isn't it?"

"Coach," Johnny said. "Tom lost a bet and had to wear a dress to tonight's hockey game. But we don't want anyone to laugh at him. So everyone else agreed to wear a dress to the game. So if they laugh at him, they laugh at the whole team."

"Everyone on the team?" Tom said.

Two more guys stepped into the dressing room. They wore dresses too.

"Everyone," Johnny said. "After all, we are a team. And that includes you, doesn't it?"

Tom thought about it for a second. He stepped forward and shook Stu's hand.

"Yes," Tom said. "And you guys were right. It is great to be on this team."

Sigmund Brouwer is the bestselling author of many books for children and young adults. Sigmund loves visiting schools and talking to children about reading and writing. *Timberwolf Chase* is the first book in the Timberwolves series. Sigmund divides his time between Red Deer, Alberta, and Eagleville, Tennessee.